Disney

This friendly book belongs to

_____

Written by K.R. Knight

BEST FRIENDS

These two friends are true friends.
"Miss Lady!" they say.
"You've got a new collar!
Well, it's a fine day!"

A muzzle's no puzzle
When best friends help out.
And now Lady's free
To go romping about!

A noodle, a strudel,
A cookie or carrot
Will taste even better
With a true friend to share it!

Let's jump and let's romp!
Come frolic and run!
For true friends want new friends
To join in the fun!

True hearts are two hearts
That love one another.
And best friends are sometimes
A father and mother.

How high we can fly!
What dreams we can dare!
When best friends team up,
They can soar anywhere!

Hello! Who are you?
And where have you been?
I'll show you around,
And you'll soon fit right in!

The day says, "Let's play!"
The world says, "I'm yours!"
Adventures await
In the big, bright outdoors.

Do friends ever ask you
To try something new?
True friends will let you
Teach them something, too!

Caring and sharing,
At playtime and rest.
A true friend like you
Is the best of the best!